The Love of Sisters

Also by Eugene McCabe

Stage plays

King of the Castle
Breakdown
Pull Down a Horseman
Gale Day
Swift

Television plays

Adapted from original prose works
A Matter of Conscience
Some Women on the Island
The Funeral
Cancer
Heritage
Siege
Music at Annahullion
Contributions to *The Riordans*

Prose

Victims (novel)
Death and Nightingales (novel)
Heritage and other Stories
Christ in the Fields (Fermanagh Trilogy)
Heaven Lies about Us (selected stories)
Cyril (A fable for children)

The Love of Sisters

Eugene McCabe (signature)

by

Eugene McCabe

NEW
ISLAND

THE LOVE OF SISTERS
First published 2009
by New Island
2 Brookside
Dundrum Road
Dublin 14

www.newisland.ie

ISBN 978-1-84840-018-4

British Library Cataloguing Data. A CIP catalogue record for this book is available from the British Library.

Book design by Inka Hagen
Printed in the UK by CPI Mackays, Chatham ME5 8TD

New Island received financial assistance from
The Arts Council (An Chomhairle Ealaíon), Dublin, Ireland.

10 9 8 7 6 5 4 3 2 1

For my sisters

Acknowledgments

My very real gratitude to Dermot Bolger who accepted this effort without hesitation. Also my sincere thanks to Tom McAlindon, a friend of fifty years plus whose reservations and suggestions included the title for this work.

Last year, his *Bloodstains in Ulster* was chosen by Bernard McLaverty in *The Irish Times* as Book of the Year. He has just published *Two Brothers, Two Wars*, a haunting memoir about war and death and the invisible bond of familial love.

I would also like to thank a younger friend, Maria Magee, for permission to use the beauty and strength of her artwork.

Finally to Deirdre O'Neill whose promptness, humour and clarity made the chore of editing both simple and agreeable.

An extract from a work in progress, *Sisters*, appeared in issue 6/volume two of *the stinging fly*, Spring 2007.

L ATE AUTUMN 1947. Muriel Carmody was scarcely a month dead when the rumours started. Carmel, the youngest, looked at times as though she'd been crying a lot. The nuns at primary school alerted the social services. Their mother's sister, Imelda, arrived from Mallow for the month's mind to find the house cold and chaotic, the kitchen filthy, her nieces unkempt, both with chilblains and living mostly on crisps, chips and cornflakes. They were taken on an extended holiday to Moytura, a large farmhouse near Mallow.

Imelda had married Tom Denehey, an agricultural contractor with a spread of land and a deep pocket. Being childless, they were more than happy to rear the girls and give them an education. Word came then that Denis Carmody had sold the family home and dental practice and was suddenly gone. America? Australia? Britain? South Africa? The depths of the sea? No one knew or cared. As this gradually became obvious, Carmel often wept, saying, 'Poor Dada, poor Dada; will we ever see him again?'

Tricia was impassive about her father. The sisters matured unalike. The elder, a Titian red-head, was quick-witted, flirtatious, more attract-ive than good-looking. The younger, fine-skinned with vulnerable eyes and black hair, was patho-logically shy and much more striking. A serious student with the Dominicans, she adapted to convent life and got excellent reports.

'*A natural scholar. Will go far,*' they com-mented.

The reports about Tricia observed, '*Very gifted. Can be facetious in class and elsewhere. Could try harder.*'

Back at Moytura on holidays, Carmel, unlike her sister, avoided dances, parties, outings and overnights. She felt uneasy in the presence of males with the exception of priests, and later, as a nun, with the Franciscan monks from an adjacent monastery who came to celebrate daily Mass and to hear confessions on Friday.

As a novice she was in a state of spiritual exaltation. When Sister Magda Reilly, the organist, played the *Ave Verum, Jesu, Joy of Man's Desiring, Abide With Me* and other sublime hymns, her eyes welled up. She loved benediction, meditation, silence and the orderly and unchanging daily timetable:

6.15 a.m.	*Office and readings followed by mental prayer*
7.45 a.m.	*The Body of Christ followed by breakfast*
10 a.m.	*Adoration and work*
11.30 a.m.	*Scripture reading*
12 p.m.	*Midday prayer followed by dinner*
2 p.m.	*Adoration and work*
3 p.m.	*Mid-afternoon prayer and office of the dead*
4 p.m.	*Rosary*
5 p.m.	*Study*
6 p.m.	*Evening prayer followed by tea and leisure time*
7.15 p.m.	*Mental prayer*
	Night prayer

Three nights a week: Office of readings at midnight.

When professing as a nun she kept her own name. Mary of Mount Carmel was not only the ancient holy place of the early Carmelites, she was also the Mother of God, the perfect disciple. It was beautiful beyond imagination to be in love with Jesus; to receive His physical body, to know without doubt that His love was reciprocated in full and that her contemplative life and that of her reclusive sisters was helping to fuel a beacon of hope in the darkness of an unhappy, sin-befuddled world.

She left when she was 26. When asked why, she would answer with one word, 'scruples'. During the limbo time that followed, she stayed with Tricia near Spanish Point. Tricia had divorced in London and got custody of her three-year-old child, Isabel. She had specialised in midwifery and thereafter spent seven years attached to a natural birth clinic near Kensington. She was happy living and working in London until the IRA bombings started. From then on, with her soft Clare accent she could sense watchfulness or hostility, sometimes both. As things worsened she decided to come home. Her only mistake over there, she said, was marrying a Welshman who welched on her for an older woman with money.

She survived comfortably with an inherited settlement and freelance nursing in a converted schoolhouse with a miraculous view of the sea. Meantime she insisted on paying Carmel generously for keeping the house and minding Isabel. She also paid for driving lessons.

'For God's sake, Sis, you've been imprisoned for the best years of your life! The car's idle every other day. I'll go with you when I can. Driving's a plus if you're looking for work.

'And if you get an emergency call?' Carmel asked.

'I'll get a taxi. I often do because of Isabel … I take her with me.'

'But that's—'

'Money! It's nothing, I'll explain sometime.'

Carmel was a quick learner. She enjoyed the freedom of being able to go anywhere in the country and was soon confident enough to take Isabel for company.

'Thanks be to God,' Tricia said one night after a third gin, 'you're out of that fishy place – ringing bells when you're half-starved, mumbling round the clock for God knows what. It's foolish … Godology praying for peace or anything else.

Nothing changes, ever.'

To which Carmel responded gently, 'We never had to ring the hungry bell and you don't understand about prayer.'

'I do,' Tricia muttered, 'but I don't know who's listening and I'm sorry, but all that reclusive stuff smells of me! me! me! and my crucified lover, the miracle man!'

Carmel was deeply hurt by this blasphemy and upset by the scepticism, but tears came to her eyes when Tricia insisted on talking almost casually about unthinkable things she said had happened after their mother died and their father came home drunk. She once cut sharply across Tricia on the edge of temper, 'I remember nothing like that!'

'Why would I make it up?'

'I don't know!'

This was blurted so emphatically that Tricia paused and said with equal emphasis, 'I *do* know. I was eight, Sis, and you were five when Aunt Mella came for us. Maybe you don't remember or don't want to. The baby-sitter? The two of them on the kitchen couch! We saw that and closed the door quietly and went upstairs. We said nothing to each other. There were no words for what we saw. You don't remember? No? There were other things. No memories?'

'Nothing.'

What really hurt was the almost throwaway, 'Can't you guess why you joined an enclosed order?'

Once during a convent visit when Carmel was a novice, she hesitantly suggested that they pray in chapel for their erring, drunken father.

'I will if you like, that he's dead and gone to hell.'

That response was like a slap in the face. Carmel recovered enough to ask, 'Have you not it in your heart to forgive, Trish?'

'Some things are unforgivable.'

Carmel was so distressed by this refusal that she avoided similar requests and remembered thinking how you can be deeply hurt by some-one but continue to love them. Now back near Spanish Point, she applied with her honours Leaving Certificate marks to the medical faculty at University College Cork and was accepted immediately for late September. When she talked about writing to the Medical Missionaries of Mary in Drogheda, Tricia had pursed her lips and shook her head vigorously, 'Just take one year's sabbatical, one year of reality.'

'But the expense! The missionaries will put me through.'

'We'll manage without them.'

'We? How?'

'I'll explain some other time. Meantime you've had enough religion for ten lifetimes.'

Carmel avoided television apart from children's afternoon programmes. In the evenings she spent her time checking the employment ads and minding Isabel. If there was useful work she could do anywhere she intended applying for it. Tricia was anxious for her to stay on at the old schoolhouse until the academic year started. One night she was startled to be told, 'I think it's safe to tell you now, Sis, you're a woman of modest means!'

Aunt Mella and Tom Denehey had died horrendously in a car accident somewhere in the south of Spain in 1965. It was surmised that Tom had had a brief lapse and was on the wrong side of the road, or maybe he'd had a heart attack. Whatever the cause, they met a lorry head on. When their remains were flown home, both were unrecognisable. The rule of the order allowed community members to attend the funerals of parents or siblings only.

Carmel, though insulated by enclosure, had been greatly saddened by the accident. She loved them both but not for a moment did she imagine she'd inherit. When Moytura and various land and share holdings were sold and divided between nephews and nieces, each got something in excess of 55,000 punts. Tricia suggested that Carmel's inheritance should not be absorbed into a religious order but kept for her in trust. It was invested in Guinness and Bank of Ireland shares. Dividends and share issues were added over the years to an account in her name. These details were sent to Tricia. The order was not advised.

'Apart from the shares, you've got quite a stash of readies. You could put yourself through college comfortably.'

'Should that not have gone to the convent?'

'Clearly not.'

'But—'

'You'd have nothing now. Where do you think I got money to glamourise this gazebo?'

Tricia tended to sleep on into the afternoon when she had to work at night. At the weekends she went golfing. She was also part of a poker school and sometimes played till three in the morning. When car wheels scrunched the yellow pea gravel, Carmel, if awake, got up to make tea. Tricia could be talkative in a slightly embarrassing way, her eyes blood-veined, her breath smelling of gin and cigarettes which she continued to smoke as she drank tea. Sometimes, using a hand mirror, she cream-cleansed her face at the kitchen table with wads of cotton wool to remove eye make-up and wipe off lipstick which she applied overmuch. Now and then Carmel tried to find out more about her experiences as a midwife.

'In the beginning,' she said, 'every birth seemed like a miracle but ... eh ...' She shrugged.

'Surely it is the greatest miracle every time?'

Tricia looked away for a moment.

'After hundreds it seems less so. There's billions and billions of us on the planet now.'

After a month or less she realised Tricia was right when she talked about the country being so profoundly changed.

Ulster was in turmoil with bombings and murders every other day. She'd never heard of

Mister Paisley. Now she could see him bellowing on television. He was wearing a Roman collar. She asked Tricia about him, 'The spiritual pope of Ulster love, born to drum his people into paradise. He suits them well, but no worse than our crozier boys down here.'

'You're not serious, Trish!'

'Power crazy and sex obsessed, most of them. Christ must hate their carry on.'

'Why do you say such unkind things about our own church?'

'They're maybe worse than I'm saying.'

When settled in, she could see that every other television programme had a reference to sexuality. Mock copulation was commonplace on screen. Magazines and popular newspapers showed girls with dangling breasts and pelvic pointing. Tricia shrugged about it,

'The young ones are at it like rabbits. They don't bother marrying now before starting families. Hundreds cross the water every year for abortions.'

'They *murder* their own children!'

'Potential children.'

'How could they do such a thing and live with themselves?'

Realising suddenly that she was condemning, she added, 'God help them.'

'God helps nobody.'

'What?'

'God's asleep since the world began and if he's awake he doesn't care what goes on down here.'

❦

ONE NIGHT Tricia mentioned that there was a parish priest in the poker school called Ultan MacCarthy. The only son of a wealthy Cork family, he was educated at Ampleforth. His accent sounded very grand to Irish ears. Carmel, attempting to be casual, asked, 'Does the canon ever ask you about not going to Mass or confession?'

Tricia blinked at her, 'Should he?'

'It's a mortal sin.'

'Are you serious?'

'Don't pretend, Trish, you know it is.'

Tricia shrugged, 'I think we both know what's mortal.' Silence and then, 'Don't we?'

That question was enough to deflect Carmel's concern about religious externals, but made her wonder how someone as generous and knowing as Tricia could be so unforgiving, so indifferent to her own morality and mortality. The shrug about her child's spiritual future was, in Carmel's view, akin to the behaviour of a blighted soul. That worried her a lot. Early on, when it was clear that Isabel had not been baptised and knew no prayers, she baptised the child in the bathroom sink and began teaching her The Novena of Our Lady of Mount Carmel which comprised an Our Father, Hail Mary and Glory Be, ending with, 'Show us that you are Our Mother and pray for us sinners, now and forever more, Amen.'

Carmel stressed that it was a secret between them. Within a week they would whisper this secret novena before the bedtime story. Isabel was told about the birth of Jesus in a crib in Bethlehem, the angel, the shepherds and the wise kings. It was too soon to tell her about His wonderful life and cruel death, that He was both man and God, the supreme ruler of the universe.

Gradually the weeks of waiting became, in a surprising way, like the early novice time of happiness and expectation in the convent. She had the old schoolhouse to herself. It had the original high windows, but the entire gable looking east was restructured with plate glass and filled with light from dawn till dusk. There was a Scandinavian wood stove which seldom went out, colourful wall hangings and a variety of rugs, knick-knacks and curiosities Tricia had picked up in London. More importantly, it had no end of books and long-playing records, jazz and classical.

Outside, the old gravelled playground had raised beds of Veronica, dune grasses and, to crown it all, Isabel was such a beautiful creature that looking into the child's eyes was like seeing the sky or sea after a long enclosure in the dark or coming across some startling phenomenon of nature. With Tricia absent delivering babies, golfing or socialising at weekends, Carmel and Isabel slept together. When the car was free they went shopping or driving along the coast. One day they went to the Burren and explored its primeval cragginess and brought a picnic. Carmel couldn't make the child understand that it was forbidden to pick the tiny, alpine-type flowers in cracks and crevices.

'Why?'

'Because it's against the law.'

'Why?'

'Because they're special and rare.'

'I hate the law.'

'You'll understand when you grow up.'

'Auntie Carmel, you're always saying that!'

'Am I?'

'And do you know everything?'

Surprised by the child's directness, she paused before answering, 'No love, no, far from, very far from, but like you I'm learning every day, with God's help.'

In the village, most customers and shop-keepers knew and greeted Isabel. The child was a buffer that made Carmel less shy. It was a joy to be able to talk to locals. She could sense from them an unspoken sympathy for her dilemma. Although she had swapped the habit and headgear of the convent for Tricia's navy cardigan, skirt and flat shoes, she was still unmistakably nunnish. Tricia had offered her the pick of two wardrobes and a chest of drawers with a variety of seasonal outfits, all of them tasteful and expensive. Carmel had refused, picking only the worn, quieter ones.

'It's not fair, Trish, they're yours; you may need them.'

'They're giveaway now, love, take what you want. What you've on is like a sign saying, "Guess what? I was a nun once upon a time!"'

The year at Spanish Point had moved on to the heartbreaking glory of May. Every morning Carmel had breakfast with Isabel in the kitchen, then brought in a tray of tea and toast to Tricia's untidy bedroom, watching the way the child put her arms round her mother, kissing her awake to suckle on one breast then the other. This bond Tricia accepted half asleep, almost unaware. As she lit a cigarette one morning she became aware of Carmel looking on with pursed lips. 'I know; it's pure laziness, but I'm no earth mother, I'll wean her soon.'

'Have you really tried?' Carmel asked.

''Course I have. Rages and tantrums every time. Be great if you could stay on, she's pure light about you, can't you tell? You're her sun, moon and stars. I'm almost jealous. I'll arrange a fortnight away; that should do it. She'll be happy with you and a bottle. Stay till she's weaned. Promise?'

Carmel nodded and asked, 'Did you win last night at the poker?'

'We all won. The canon stood the party.

He's got pucks of it from his own family and an American aunt. He's a fussy cook, no housekeeper, keeps a French polisher who gets a bed and the run of his teeth for shining furniture, a very attractive lad. He got him from an orphanage somewhere.'

'Saint Don Bosco,' Carmel said, 'was wonderful with poor street boys.'

Tricia stared at her sister, thinking she's still gullible, still knows nothing, absolutely nothing about the real world, then heard herself say, 'Yes, that's possible, I suppose, the French polishing.'

Tricia also knew that one of the confirmed miracles was the saint's tendency to levitate while saying Mass. She resisted the temptation to ask, 'Why? How often? How high?'

Carmel had no evident sense of humour. The same growing up. When jokes had to be explained she pronounced them 'silly'. When Tricia told her that she lacked humour, Carmel replied she was glad of that lack. Girls her own age, she said, seemed to talk and giggle about nothing much but clothes, shoes and things sexual. The young men they whispered about she thought ridiculous. She'd once overheard a group of them boasting about the pints they'd drunk the night before. It occurred to her at the time that they'd probably grow into portly men like her big-bellied father. In the silence that followed, Tricia suddenly asked, 'Do you take dreams seriously, Sis?'

'Depends. They can be disturbing.'

'Being alive is stranger than being dead. Sometimes I imagine it must be all right to be gone wherever we go, or don't go. Death everlasting, don't you think?'

'No. I hope to see God and His Mother and our mother and father and all our kin and "the joy that is not of this world".'

All the time they'd been talking, Carmel was aware of teeth marks on Tricia's neck. She'd seen them before she'd entered the convent on a girl's neck at breakfast after a teenage party at Moytura. When she'd asked innocently what they were, the girl had answered with an embarrassed shrug, 'Have you never seen a love bite or had one?'

Later that morning in the bathroom mirror Tricia saw what Carmel saw and muttered, 'Oh Jesus no!', then in dialect, 'Blasht!'

She carefully concealed the marks with a

blue silk scarf. Willie Griffin, a golfing friend, was clerk of the court and an economics lecturer in Limerick. His wife had left him, blaming him for her empty womb. Tricia sometimes slept with him if both felt inclined. They were loving friends, no more than that. It was no business of Carmel's to be handed such details, but no doubt she'd be thinking of her now as a kind of Magdalen and praying for her at the kitchen sink.

In fact she was at the sink window beside Isabel who was standing on a chair helping her aunt to dry the breakfast things. Carmel turned and smiled with no hint of accusation and Tricia thought, what clear eyes, what perfect skin and glossy hair. Years of physical and spiritual diet in a nunnery? No booze, no fags, no perfume, no sex, no make-up and a crystal-clear conscience, and now that she was months out of the convent garden her raw, roughened hands had become elegant and beautiful again. Suddenly Tricia was conscious of the perfume on her silk scarf, the lipstick and mascara, her foundation-powdered face, padded bra and the fine cotton blouse revealing a marked cleavage. To disguise a feeling of miniscule shame, she lifted Isabel from the chair, tickling her and making growling noises. That deflection always made the child laugh almost hysterically.

❧

ONE NIGHT when Carmel imagined she was dreaming she woke to find Isabel suckling. She switched on the bedside lamp and gently prized the mouth away from her breast. The child half opened her glazed eyes, 'I'm sorry, darling, I've no milk.'

'Why?'

'Because I've no baby.'

'Why?'

'Because I never married.'

'Why?'

'Because I was a nun.'

'Have nuns no babies?'

'No. Go back to sleep love.'

She lay awake till dawn. The following morning Tricia said, 'Your eyes look inflamed.'

'Conjunctivitis. I've had it before,' Carmel said.

Tricia looked at her sister intently, then asked, 'Are you troubled about something, Sis?

20

Can we talk?'

'It's nothing,' Carmel said again. 'I'll get something from the chemist.'

The beach was a favourite place. They gathered shells, odd-shaped stones and coloured glass smoothed by sand and sea. Carmel now understood fully the Solomon story about how the woman who smothered her child accidentally could be desolate enough to claim another's. It was such a different love to the love of God so carefully nurtured in the convent. It was also a time for her to think about the years of enclosed prayer and contemplation and her reasons for leaving. There was a part of her that didn't want to dwell on why she had left. Up to the moment of leaving she was uncertain about her motives.

The more she put off thinking about it the more some disturbing details pushed themselves to the front of her mind. At times she was afraid of falling asleep because of images intruding on her unconscious.

✄

HER FIRST experience as a raw novice had been humbling. Sister Magda Reilly, a nun in her late seventies, was choir organist and an exceptional musician who sometimes entertained them in their free time with recitals of Chopin, Schubert, Mozart and popular music from American musicals if Mother Bernard Barrett, the abbess, was away. Magda's illness began with blinding headaches. Migraine, the community said, but when she started to sing and talk incoherently, sometimes crawling under the bed, the doctor was sent for. Carmel's task was to ring a cast iron hand bell from the hall door, warning other sisters that a male body was in the house. She led Dr Fitzgerald to Magda's cell door.

As they opened the door Magda was giggling and muttering at the window about the red hot pokers in Sister Martha's garden and how her bottom had 'scorch marks from the devil's prick. God's truth, God's truth, God's truth!'

Deeply embarrassed, Mother Bernard introduced her to Fitzgerald, who asked gently, 'Would you like to tell us what's troubling you, Sister?'

Turning from the window, her eyes red from crying, Magda whispered, 'I am the shite of the world, that's my only trouble.'

'And why do you think that?'

She turned away with a headshake. To further questions from Fitzgerald, she again shook her head.

Out in the bare, big-windowed corridor, Bernard said apologetically, 'It's utterly out of character doctor, utterly. She's the gentlest creature imaginable. God alone knows where that language comes from.'

Fitzgerald said, 'The playground most likely,' then added quietly, 'The mind has mountains.'

'How would you diagnose?'

'I'm not sure – dementia? A growth possibly. Whatever it is, it's not good.'

'What do you suggest doctor?'

'A psychiatrist first, perhaps?'

When he was gone, Bernard asked, 'What was that about mountains, Carmel?'

'I think it's Manley Hopkins, Mother, the Jesuit poet.'

'Of course.'

Again Carmel had to open the door to the psychiatrist from Limerick Mental, a fattish man in a brown tweed suit with round lenses on the end of his bulbous nose. He had a tangle of reddish hair and an unkempt beard, and Carmel thought he looked like a kindly teddy bear until he spoke. The voice was glacial, the accent Scottish, 'What's the bell for?'

'To let the sisters know, Doctor.'

'Know what?'

'That you're here.'

'Why should they know that?'

'It's a rule of the house.'

'Ridiculous bloody rule. Stop that racket.'

Accustomed to authority and immediate obedience, Carmel had caught the bell clapper. As they approached a stone staircase in silence, she heard the psychiatrist say, 'I'm no leper.'

Mother Bernard was on the first landing. A higher civil servant with a late vocation, she generated more fear than affection. A tall woman, she was standing beside Magda's cell door in a white fury, her hooded eyes unreadable. Over and above Magda's crazy singing and rambling, she'd clearly overheard the last remark. As they approached she said, articulating each word sharply, 'Sister Carmel, ring that man back down to the front door and show him out.'

The psychiatrist blinked, then responded by jerking his thumb towards Magda's cell, 'You've a very sick woman in there.'

As he turned to leave, he said, 'You'll get a bill tomorrow from Doctor Robert Gault for travel and a stupid waste of time.'

'It won't be paid, Sir.'

'Then I'll sue.'

'We'll sue back. How dare you mock the rules of this house! Walk ahead, Sister. Ring that person out, all the way. Show him the street immediately.'

Carmel led him back down the wide stone staircase and along the high-ceilinged corridors, bell ringing as she walked ahead. She felt foolish. Putting the bell on a table to unbolt and unlock the massive door, she heard Gault say, 'Thon big bossy cow's in dire need of treatment herself.'

Mother Bernard phoned Limerick again and asked for a female psychiatrist. Magda was confined and heavily sedated for a month in Mulgrave Street Mental. She came back looking estranged and weeping a lot. She kept telling everyone she was a great sinner. She'd lost her appetite and appeared shrunken. From osteosarcoma, she'd developed over the years a disfiguring hump. Referring to it sometimes, she whispered to Carmel, 'A judgement of God for my sins, child, despair and doubt. Those two breed the devil's hump.'

'That's nonsense, Magda. You're the kindest and the holiest person in the house.'

Lacking motivation and energy, Magda kept to her cell, staring at the ceiling or out her window at the sky. Part of Carmel's duties was to attend to the old nun's food and functions. She tried not to take in what her eyes saw while giving her a bed bath. On the evening of her seventieth birthday, Magda was markedly low, her eyes closed as she said in less than a whisper, 'I wonder in God's name why I was ever born into this world?'

Carmel had answered brightly, 'That's a dark thought, Magda. This is your birthday, a day for rejoicing!'

'It's my death day. Thanks be to God.'

The old nun's eyes were closed. She'd been anointed last Tuesday for the second time. No point in sending for the priest again. She pointed a long forefinger at her ear. Carmel knelt to listen as the words came brokenly, struggling between painful, uncertain breathing as though determined to say what was in her head before departure, indistinct at the start but growing in clarity and intensity. Carmel caught the opening gist and certainly her final words. It was as though she'd been rehearsing them for years. There was no way now of stopping her to clarify.

'God help me ... baby oil he used and never a word since ... married in Boston, so I heard ... not even his children's names ... my nieces, nephews, and me locked up here, my head in a twist ... "dry rot of the soul", a Jesuit told me in the box, "pray daughter pray", but I couldn't pray ... my heart went cold towards God and stayed that way ... only Jesus Christ knows why ... and it was sore so it was ....but still and all I'll not be lonesome anymore with my sisters down the garden in the ground...

... blind to stars and swallows and the sun...
...thanks be to God it's at an end ... at last ...
...We'll all be together in ...
...God's acre ... forgotten.'

The chilling clarity of these confessional words ceased suddenly at the word 'forgotten'. As the rattle started, Carmel, partly in shock at what she'd heard or imagined she'd heard, began whispering an act of contrition, begging God to receive Magda's troubled soul into paradise with love, forgiveness and mercy. As she did so, Magda pushed her head back deep into her pillow, thrust up both arms and uttered a howl so loud, so unexpected, so inhuman, that Carmel felt her heart judder suddenly then begin racing painfully as she caught Magda's bony wrists to absorb whatever it was that had caused the unnerving utterance. The nuns, carrying the candle-lit cake to the sick bay and singing 'Happy Birthday', heard the chilling shriek and fell silent. When they arrived and saw Magda's staring eyes, wide open mouth and Carmel crying, they blew out the cake candles and circled the bed on their knees saying the rosary, in shock and tears. Sister Martha closed Magda's eyes by placing two brass sink plugs on them, then closed her gaping mouth by inserting a small statue of Saint Christopher under her chin.

No one wanted to ask about the unnerving howl. All wanted to know her parting words, 'A jumble mostly,' Carmel prevaricated, 'something about swallows and stars.'

'That's beautiful,' they murmured, 'so

Magda, like her music.'

'She had a happy death.'

'Pure innocence … may God be good to her.'

'Well she's with Jesus now at the end of all.'

'How could she suffer like she did and not be with Jesus at the end of all?'

Apart from preparing her dead sisters for burial, Sister Martha Quigley was also head gardener. She was a blunt Cavan woman, a lay sister who used her earthy dialect with no concessions to convent elocution or grammar. At the moment she needed help and asked, 'Carmel, you can give me a hand here?'

Mother Bernard Barrett intervened quietly, 'I think maybe Carmel's been through enough this last week and these last few hours.'

'Enough what? Sure we'll all die, Mother. Are you game to help girl?'

Carmel said promptly, 'Yes, I'd like to.'

Bernard nodded with smiling dignity as though giving way to a whim of contrariness. The community knew Martha was the only sister who dared question Bernard's authority. Amongst themselves they said, 'Mother Bernard's our abbess, but Martha's the real boss.'

Everyone knew Martha had a whip-like tongue to match Bernard's. Often they were in the office, their heads together, going over accounts and correspondence. They understood each other and were never heard to clash. Martha was conscious of being privy to knowledge unknown to the rest of the community. One winter's evening a sheet of *The Cork Examiner* was whipped by a sudden gust high over the garden wall and came to rest at her feet. She knew all reading matter but religious literature was forbidden. In the normal course she'd have crumpled it for the compost heap, but an irresistible headline caught her eye.

BARRETT'S MODEL FARM AT NEW ROSS
FOR SALE
JUDGE CURTAYNE REFUSES REMISSION
PLEA

The case had to do with a plea arising from events of two years back. She looked around. It was near dark and Gemma, her sister helper, had left the garden. She took the sheet to the polytunnel and put on her glasses, feeling like an eavesdropper as she read guiltily in the half-light with increased heartbeat and welling eyes. She gathered that Bernard's brother Bartholomew had sold 37 purebred Aberdeen Angus cattle certified by his vet son Jeremy as free from tuberculosis and contagious abortion. Within months 36 of the cows were discovered to be diseased. A case in the High Court followed. The only healthy animal and the most expensive of the draft sale was a female heifer, twin to a bull with the genital malformation of all Free Martins. The heifer had damaged a valuable bull's penis when service was attempted.

The sale of the 700-acre farm with all machinery and the purebred Angus herd at Model Farm failed to cover legal costs or compensate the farmers who had bought and brought contamination to their farms and very likely to the farms of their neighbours. It mentioned that Jeremy Barrett had been struck off the professional register of veterinary surgeons and had emigrated to Britain with his wife and three daughters. He was rumoured to be working on a building site.

It was almost incredible, the judge concluded, that two intelligent men on a farm ironically called Model Farm could calculate to

inflict anything so dishonest, callous and irre-
sponsible to the welfare and income of their
fellow farmers and indeed to the livestock
health of the nation. He refused remission of
the five-year sentence imposed on Barrett and
said if the law allowed he would be inclined to
increase it.

Martha was overwhelmed by this knowledge and surprised that Bernard had never
once alluded to this family shame, which must
have caused her continual grieving, especially
the exile and disgrace of her nephew, his wife
and three nieces and what Bernard referred to
dismissively as 'Bartle's poor creature, Abigail'.
Martha had seen them sitting on a garden seat
talking with quiet intensity about two years
back, a heavily made-up woman with glazed
eyes and a downturned, luridly lipsticked
mouth.

As head gardener Martha associated daily
with Bernard who once mentioned that she
slept badly this past while and seemed on the
edge of intimating something personal,
changed her mind, smiled her cold smile and
said, 'Martha I don't know what I'd do without
you, you're a tower of strength.'

She said this often because Martha kept the community in eggs, milk, pork, chicken, potatoes, fresh and frozen vegetables, fruits and greens, honey from 30 hives, preserves, jams and chutneys all the year round. Being responsible for the three-acre walled-in garden and orchard, she was exempt from the strict convent schedule. Forbidden to associate with males, she used a go-between called Virgy O'Meara. Virgy dealt with the collection and delivery to and from the convent garden store, an old coach house that gave directly on to a back street of the town now stretching as far as the garden walls. She had a second-hand Morris minor van brightened with hand-painted sunflowers. How she made cash from this trade was not clear, but her purse was always fat. A whippet of a woman, she often smelled of brandy imbibed, Martha suspected, when collecting pub beer waste for Martha's endless war of attrition, the drowning of slugs. Compulsive and indiscreet, Martha knew more about her than she wished to.

She had two children by her sister's husband Willie Fitch, a prospering cattle dealer. Both families celebrated Christmas and children's birthdays together. Martha found this arrangement difficult to understand. She kept the knowledge of it to herself, knowing Bernard wouldn't approve. Indispensable to the convent economy, Virgy scoured the shops, supermarts, hotels, pubs and bakeries to garner goods past their sell-by date. If doubtful, these perishables were fed to the few pigs and laying hens. Mostly they were safely eaten by the community. Every July there was a successful open-day sale organised by voluntary female workers to sell the excess jams and chutneys from the kitchen store plus a variety of potting plants, needle and basketry work and a selection of Limerick lace. Without Martha's thriving garden and Virgy's contacts, they could in theory be forced to the humiliation of ringing the hungry bell to let the outside world know they were close to starving. This had never happened during Martha's watch of 30 years.

When Bernard was away, Martha was in charge. She had the name of being difficult to work with. As no men were allowed within the precincts of the house or garden, she had to call on younger, more able-bodied nuns to help with emergency digging, potting, planting out, fruit harvesting and winter storage. It was an arduous undertaking for an ageing, burly woman in her mid-fifties. She seemed well able for it and was not given to complaining. She gave directions now to Carmel.

'Strip the poor cratur and don't let them pillows get soiled with slobber. Put a towel under them. I'll get the rubber sheet and paraphernalia. You fetch a basin, soap and water.'

Left alone, Carmel got what Martha had ordered, then removed the pillows and regulation nightdress. The crooked arthritic hands were folded modestly over her crotch. Carmel stared, asking herself *how?* She had placed the lifeless arms under the quilt. Had they moved by some unknown mechanism to cover her modesty? Without experience she was uncertain about the ring of profession and the gold chain with its miraculous medal, a jubilee gift from a wealthy, anonymous member of Opus Dei. Hard now to imagine, she thought, anything more nothing than this scarcely human thing on the bed, naked, hunchbacked with stick-like arms and legs, the two pathetic withered breasts like small, wrinkled sausages lying sideways beside the grey fuzz of each armpit. This, she thought, is what I'll be some day, this thing, this nothing, this poor remnant of a life of prayer, work and meditation. She was relieved to hear Martha bustling down the corridor.

'Off with the ring, girl, and medal and chain. We'll have to measure her.'

'Measure? She's tiny, Martha.'

'That hump has her like a half hoop, we don't want her head bangin' off the lid. They might think she was knockin' to get out, specially after that howl she let.'

Carmel held the tape taut from head to toe as Martha measured the middle drop with an extension rule.

'She'll fit, just. We can stick a go of foam rubber at her head before we bolt her down and plant her. What was thon howl about? Put the heart across me and I seen some of the others go white as ghosts.'

'A sudden piercing pain, Martha … she clutched at her stomach.'

'I never heerd the lek, God help us all.'

Martha then lifted Magda like a baby while Carmel covered the mattress with a rubber sheet.

'Watch this now, girl, and you'll be fit to get me ready next week if Jesus gives me the nod!'

Martha slipped on long-sleeved rubber gloves and in a few minutes the functional orifices were packed with cotton wool, the nose well sealed by pushing wool high into each nostril with a tweezers. They washed and dried her, fitted a blue shroud and fixed the cooling fingers to clasp the wooden convent-made rosary beads with its figureless cross.

'That's poor Magda now, washed for the box and ready for takeoff.'

Carmel suddenly found herself sobbing. Martha's muscular arm was round her shoulder as she asked, 'Did you love her that much girl?'

For a while Carmel couldn't or didn't want to tell Martha why she was crying, until finally she said, 'I was thinking of my own mother and father.'

'Both gone?'

Carmel nodded.

'That's hard, lassie, very hard. Fambley?'

'One sister, Tricia, and her daughter. I love them so much.'

'Of course you do, of course you do.'

Martha squeezed her arm and said, 'You'll

be all right girl; you've got heart and bravery. There's harder things than death, far harder. You'll find that out soon enough.'

My heart went cold towards God and stayed that way.

What a terrible thing to imagine – no hope, no happiness, no love, no heaven. The emptiness and loneliness of such a life haunted Carmel's memory and dreams, conjuring images she found hard to deal with. Awake or asleep, the memory of that dying howl persisted. Could it have been the devil, through that most gifted and gentle of creatures, confessing that her entire life was false, worthless? Or was it a subtle temptation to undermine her own unshakeable faith? Magda could not really have meant those bleak words after such a long life of disciplined enclosure. Or could she?

෴

CARMEL WAS four years a professed contemplative when Martha asked her one January evening if she'd ever used a spade. Her assistant Gemma was exhausted and down with flu. Carmel said she'd never had the opportunity to use a spade.

'Would you lek to try, girl?'

'I'd love to, be a big change from a crochet needle!'

She was warned by other sisters that the idea of the garden was appealing, but that working with Martha the closest thing to voluntary torture. Thus began the two hardest and happiest years of her convent life. The old Victorian glasshouse, long since rotted, had been replaced by a capacious, plastic polytunnel. There were thirty beehives to be checked and topped up with sugar syrup, the empty ones scrupulously steamed and scoured. If it was raining, they worked in the polytunnel, potting what seemed like an endless variety of seeds and cuttings for the vegetable garden or for selling, turning over the large compost heaps or making willow wall supports which were in great demand for their open day in July. They didn't talk during this work except to clarify what had to be done, the how and the why. For Carmel it was agreeable, meditative work. On bright, dry days they dressed like Michelin men, wearing mittens and fleece-lined rubber boots and polar headgear. Even so the cold could be so intense and the work so hard that Carmel sometimes thought she'd have to give up and beg to go back to work in the house, especially when Martha was preparing potato ground, a half an acre of it, working steadily, digging and bending to lift weeds for burning. She was like a machine and merciless as a machine, pointing sternly to missed scutch tendrils or half-pulled docks. That meant digging down for the root. No half measures. Thirty years older than Carmel, she seemed to have twice the strength and energy.

After a few weeks Carmel's blistered hands toughened and roughened. She found herself gradually growing stronger. They stopped twice a day to have tea in the polytunnel. Martha buttered a kitchen loaf thickly then sprinkled it with caster sugar, saying, 'No engine runs on empty!'

These morning and afternoon breaks were supposed to be contemplative or devoted to spiritual reading. Martha usually sat in a wicker chair under a rug and sometimes slept. Carmel read. Occasionally they gave themselves a dispensation to talk. One morning Carmel asked, 'What made you join, Martha?'

'I'd no choice, girl.'

'What?'

She stared straight at Carmel from the green fearless eyes in her weathered face, as though uncertain about where to begin or whether to begin. Then suddenly she was talking.

'We lived in a cottage, Lord Farnham's estate near Cavan. My auld fella had a job with him, forest work, poor pay but better than the dole, free timber, free milk and our own wee garden of spuds. Them were big things, and a slate roof but no runnin' water. Then the mother got stomach pains. We'd no money for a doctor. A dirty appendix, they tauld us afterwards. I was ten when she went to Jesus.'

'And your family?'

'Two brothers, Tim and Cormac, in Amerikay now. After the funeral the parish priest come out and said I'd have go into the Poor Clare orphanage, a big barracks of a place in the middle of Cavan town.'

'Why?'

'No woman body in the house, clergy wouldn't allow that.'

'What! Why?'

'That was the way of it in them days; had to

be a woman body in the house, a proper wife. So in I went.'

'And no one objected?'

'To a parish priest! Have a titter of wit girl!'

'That's a worse story than mine, Martha.'

'Sure most of the country was that way them days. That's why I took the veil.'

'But you did have a vocation?'

'For certain sure none for the life *we* had, hand to mouth and the clatter of half-starved childer, and what kind of a man would have taken a fancy to a lump lek me? From an orphanage? No dowry, no nothin'?'

'A lucky man.'

'Goin' to dances, is it? In high heels, is it? In a frock and frilly knickers, all painted up to the jaws! Ah, come on now girl, don't be makin' a cod of me. I was glad to quit the hardship of home and gladder again to quit Cavan town.'

'Why did they send you down here?'

Carmel was startled by a sudden mist in Martha's eyes as she shook her head, suddenly emotional, 'That's one story I'll never tell.'

❧

MONTHS PASSED. Carmel had brought Thomas Merton's *Elected Silence* down the garden to read during tea breaks. He was like a mix of Augustine and Thomas A. Kempis. She especially liked the closing lines of the Hopkins lyric from which he'd taken the title and began to use them as a prayer mantra when tempted to anger or assailed by doubt.

I have asked to be where no storms come
Where the green swell is in the havens dumb
And out of the swing of the sea

One evening in April she was aware of Martha watching.

'You lek that book, girl? You're readin' it again.'

'It's wonderful Martha, so truthful.'

'I mind it read out a brave while back.'

'Did you like it?'

'To be straight I don't mind it much, a bit high falutin' for me. There was a whole wheen of converts after the war and no end of books about how they found God or how God found them. They were all read out loud in the refectory.'

'Fascinating.'

'Aye, surely enough, it was, it was. In the end

43

God found that poor Merton monk in Bangkok.'

'What?'

'He was out for a talk with the Dally Lammy.'

'Who?'

'He's a breed of pope out there, the Dally Lammy?'

'The Dalai Lamai? Oh he's like Mother Teresa, a living saint.'

'That's what they all said. Anyway they had their talk. The Merton monk went back to his hotel in Bangkok, plugged in his razor and fell down dead.'

'A heart attack?'

'No. The razor. Electric. A short.'

Carmel was startled by the banality of such a death and only half heard Martha go on to say, 'Back in the fifties poor Sister Agnes went the same way.'

'Shaving!'

'No! no child! She put a steel knife in a toaster and that was the end of her.'

'Good God!'

'Aye. God's good surely, but you'd wonder to yourself what's in his head. He must take odd notions betimes.'

And again Carmel wondered if Martha was pulling her leg or saying the opposite of what she was really thinking.

The walled garden was rabbit-proof, but grey squirrels, jackdaws magpies and rats Martha shot, trapped and poisoned without mercy and she was a deadly shot. Cats she terrorised with stones and shouts. Like magpies and daws they robbed the nests of starlings and swallows. Slugs she drowned with beer waste from pubs. Through the winter the garden was hung with peanut feeders for resident tits and finches. A pet robin called de Valera fed out of her hand.

There was pleasant work through April to May, erecting the long apex of ash-rod rows for French beans, cutting back the deadwood of loganberries, thinning damson trees and pruning the centre of the high standard Bramleys already old when the convent was bought in 1876 from a defunct Anglo-Irish family, its mock Roman statues and cast-iron grandiose family motifs replaced by a Virgin grotto, the elaborate fountain with its imitation Venus de Milo levelled to represent a crucifixion scene.

Carmel did the climbing on a double 16-foot ladder, following Martha's cutting instructions shouted from below. On wet days in the polytunnel they put manners on the sprawling vines – figs, peaches and apricots – with secateurs. The apricot blossom was so astonishingly beautiful it was difficult to work and not keep looking at it. Martha wouldn't allow a sprig of it for the altar.

'That's two pounds of fruit girl. God sees that blossom out here and we'll have an extra pound of apricot jam next winter to eat or for sale!' Then she added, 'By right it should be goin' out to Africa to the medical missionaries. They do powerful work out there. You could have been one of them. You have the brains.'

'I've often thought about how their work is prayer.'

One afternoon Martha said, 'Them buggers is back. They've my heart scalded.'

'Them buggers', Carmel knew were rats. Martha had a soft spot for Saint Francis, but none whatsoever for his 'brother rat'.

Carmel was familiar with the poisoning routine. She had to fill about a dozen clay land pipes with Warfarin and place them strategically.

The rats that missed the land-pipe poison ended up in cages baited with lard that had been laced with sugared strychnine.

'I'd as lief feed them a dacent last supper as drown them in a bucket.'

Her talk was so full of unconscious irreverence that Carmel asked at a morning break, 'What do you really believe, Martha?'

'That's the quare cheeky question to put to a professed nun. How am I supposed to answer?'

'Simply, like me. I believe in the Creed.'

'Sure our heads are crammed night and day with the Creed, prayers, rosaries and novenas.'

'That's no answer, Martha.'

'What was the question again, girl?'

'What do you really believe?'

She pointed over at a flutter of finches and blue tits feeding, then up to swallows and starlings soaring down to build in hollows of the red-brick garden walls.

'See them wee fellas from Africa. Come and go every year. They're miracles, every one of them. God's craturs. I believe in them and I pray to God our work'll do some good and that we'll not go hungry and that that

Cromwell man won't come back with his Protestants to murder and burn us out. I'll live by the rule till I die and then hope for the best.'

'The best?'

'Wait and see … or not see. What else can a body do, and sure who knows? It's no great matter is it?'

'Oh it's a very great matter, Martha, a very, very great matter! How can you say that? We're promised resurrection and life everlasting. We're promised paradise by Jesus himself.'

'True enough, true enough; this garden's paradise enough for me manetime, but if there's a better one upstairs I'll dig away goodo till I get up there.'

She had a twinkle in her eye, a half-smile on her lips. Carmel wanted to tell her she was more a kind of sceptical pantheist than a contemplative Christian nun, but knew Martha would dance rings round her for using fancy words. In any case, how could someone so kindly, so hard-working, so full of common sense and earthy irony be other than welcomed into paradise. Did Jesus have a sense of humour? she wondered.

༃

DURING THE post-Christmas season of her second year working in the garden, Carmel dreamt one night about how Jesus loved all women. Mary Magdalen the sinner had anointed His feet with precious oils, weeping as she dried them with her hair. Some day in heaven Carmel would splash her own tears on those divine feet. He would put a hand under her chin, lift her face, look into her eyes and no earthly love could equal that infinite gaze. Then she began to wonder did He gaze into the eyes of millions and millions of girls, women, arthritic grannies, spinsters and old withered hunchbacked nuns like Magda, diseased, repentant prostitutes? And what then? And what then? And what then after all the gazing? Bury her head in his lap to inhale that smell of maleness and as she did so she woke suddenly with a leakage of blood and an ache so intense that she cried out. For a few moments she lay trembling until it eased then she realised what it was. She washed away the blood, put on a pad, a dressing gown and went down to the chapel to pray that her dream was not lewd or offensive to God.

The red glow of the sanctuary lamp was

like a blessing. She lit a night light on a reading kneeler and turned to chapter XXV of *The Imitation of Christ*. As she read it and some other portions, solace and peace began to pervade her, body and soul.

All that is not of God shall perish. Be mindful of the profession thou hast made and have always before the eyes of thy soul the remembrance of thy Savior crucified. Without care and diligence thou shalt never see the face of God.

The face of God. As these words scoured the debris of impurity from her soul she heard the hinge of the chapel door, then slippered steps coming up the aisle. Whoever it was did not go to a front kneeler but sat midway in silence. A troubled novice?

It would be unseemly to leave immediately. She waited a few minutes, snuffed out the night light, genuflected to the sacred presence in the tabernacle and turned, glancing instinctively as she neared the sleepless visitor. It was Maeve Marron, a novice. Carmel smiled and nodded.

As she passed, Maeve leaned out and caught her hand.

'I have to talk to you, Carmel,' she said, moving sideways in the pew to make room. Carmel was too surprised to resist.

'I can't sleep.'

'That happens us all some nights.'

'It's more than that … Oh God, you've no idea how much more.'

As Maeve was holding her now with both hands, Carmel could sense she was being forced to sit and listen to something she'd rather not hear. She was relieved when Maeve told her she'd been down to the pantry and eaten a wedge of cooking chocolate and a spoon of honey.

'Lots of novices do that. It's normal enough till you get used to the diet.'

'Did you do that, Carmel, as a novice, go down to the pantry?'

'I thought of it often but … '

'You didn't?'

'No.'

In the half-light, half-dark, Maeve's eyes were round and luminous.

'I've something I must tell you. On my way back I saw you come in here. I stood outside for ages and then I thought, I'll tell her; I have to tell her.'

Carmel waited. Maeve's hands were hot and clammy.

'I can't sleep, Carmel, because I can't get you out of my head and the more I pray the more you're part of me, body and soul.'

Maeve's grip had tightened. Her face was so close Carmel could smell the chocolate from her breath.

'I love you, Carmel, more than God, more than myself, more than anything I've ever seen or dreamed of in the whole world and God help me I've sinned … imagining you.'

Carmel was so startled, embarrassed and revulsed by this confession that she found it difficult not to withdraw gently from Meave's grip. She was aware that to do this would be an unfeeling rejection of something she didn't understand or want to understand. It was a while before she heard herself say, as quietly as possible, 'That was a great pity, Maeve.'

'I know, I know, I know, but I'm in love desperately … and now I can't receive Jesus at Mass and everyone will know I've sinned. What'll I do, Carmel?'

'Say you've got a migraine, stay in bed. In two days you can confess and be forgiven and begin again. We all sin this way or that.'

Suddenly Maeve began to tremble before sobbing out of control, leaning against Carmel, who withdrew from the grip and put an arm around her cautiously, saying, 'Hush child, hush, hush' as though to an infant. They were hushing and sobbing thus when they became aware of a dark figure standing beside them in the aisle. It was Mother Bernard. They could sense rather than see the severity of her presence. They were in no doubt when she spoke, 'Go to your cells. I'll talk to you both after breakfast, separately.'

It was, Carmel thought, like being in infants again. As she walked back up to her cell she could feel anger growing to temper as her stomach tightened against the callous, almost inhuman, way Bernard had dealt with what was clearly a crisis of guilt and conscience. When 'heartless old cow' occurred in Carmel's head she immediately quenched it with a prayer of submission and a request to be forgiven for such ill-tempered thinking. She had no idea whatsoever that Maeve Marron had been obsessed with her. She found it hard to go back to sleep.

Carmel was not called after breakfast to Mother Bernard's office. It was as if the night scene in the chapel had never occurred. There was no sign of Maeve Marron. At the first opportunity Carmel went to her cell. It was bare, the bedclothes and sheets folded, the mattress covered with polythene. No matter how foolish or intemperate Maeve's declaration and behaviour had been, it was hard to grasp that she was suddenly gone. No farewells. Nothing. Gone.

Christ spoke continuously about the importance of love. Surely a wise abbess could have listened and reiterated what they all knew, that the physical can be sublimated by the spiritual. It was as if Maeve Marron had never existed. The sisters talked among themselves that evening during free time about the suddenness of Maeve's leavetaking. Mother Bernard explained it away with five words, 'The child was unhappy here.'

That afternoon Bernard had nodded Carmel into her office.

'Maeve spoke to me about her problem. Apart from the thieving, which we suspected she had no emotional control over, she was entirely unsuited to contemplative life. I didn't ask her to leave. I want you to understand that, Carmel. It was her own decision.'

Carmel wanted to say, 'I don't believe one word you're saying', and for an instant she was tempted to add, 'You're insulting me with lies … I'm not stupid!'

For the first time ever she kept looking straight back into those dark, hooded eyes with no sense of fear and something akin to dislike verging on hatred. She left the office so abruptly that Bernard called after her sharply, 'Sister Carmel, come back here!'

She kept walking, aware that deliberate disobedience to an abbess was a pathway to possible expulsion. There was no question now of going out to help Martha. She thought of the chapel, changed her mind and went to the convent parlour where her anger seemed to deepen. The long panelled room, originally a family library, had high shelves of books locked behind bevelled glass panels that were never opened. The room was empty except for Sister Veronica McMahon who was 87 and allowed the use of this quiet room any time she pleased. Still alert and compis mentis, she was knitting slowly and looked up through thick lenses to see Carmel, near tears, standing at the reading table. She beckoned. Carmel went towards her, aware that Veronica had rejected hearing aids, declaring them 'a noisy nuisance', and though deaf as a post always tried to lip read. Her misinterpretations caused great mirth during the evening free time.

'What is it child?'

'I'm leaving.'

'Grieving? For what dear?'

'Everything.'

'That time of the month, is it?'

Startled, Carmel nodded.

'Hated that as a novice … dreaming of infants every other night at the breast – can be hard that. Sit here beside me.'

Carmel pulled over a low stool. Veronica took her hand.

'Look what *I'm* at here … knitting pink and blue matinees. In the end it's what we spend our lives at … day in day out at this, that and the other until *that* day comes or *that* night.'

She paused. 'I used to teach the novices how to crochet till my fingers went crooked.'

'You taught me.'

'I did? Of course, yes, I remember, you were a beauty and quick to learn. I published a book on Limerick lace long ago.'

'I've seen it, Vron, it's a very special book.'

'What's wrong, dear?'

The kindness of the old woman, the uncanny intuition of her question and sympathetic owl-like stare caused Carmel's eyes to well.

'Oh dear, oh dear, oh dear, poor morsel, make yourself a tea of raspberry leaves and go to your cell. It's terrible to be young. At my age nothing matters much except when I break wind; *I* can't hear it but I see others smiling … and now you're smiling … can't be all that bad. Quit the grieving child; tomorrow it'll all seem like nothing.' Carmel's heart was still pumping painfully from the encounter with Bernard and fear of the dark roadway ahead. A voice in her head kept repeating, 'What am I going to do, what am I going to do, where am I going to go?' To further distract the young nun, Veronica pointed an arthritic finger at the portraits of two bishops hanging over the ornate black marble fireplace: one of them was wearing a purple skull cap and cape, the other gold mitered with a golden cape and crozier.

'Those lads are gone to their reward. Kissed their rings on bended knee, so I did, when I was abbess here once upon a time. Don't look all that happy, do they?'

'Is there such a thing?'

'Again, dear?'

'Happiness,' Carmel repeated loudly. 'Is there such a thing?'

''Course there is girl — our reward hereafter for hard work, prayer, and good works, nothing much else is there … within these walls or without them.'

Between the shelves on one side of the fireplace there was a smiling oleograph of Pope John XXIII. Bernard was once heard to murmur 'It's a pity he's so fat'. On the other side there was a painting of John F. Kennedy donated by a wealthy Irish-American lady after the assassination. Permission from The Federal Mother General to display this image was reluctantly granted for one year of mourning in the convent parlour. Thereafter it was to be returned to the donor or donated to a hospital, museum or some such public building. The painting had been copied from an iconic photograph taken during his visit to the home place in Wexford. It caught him holding a cup of tea casually like a glass, the cup handle cocked out. He was smiling naturally at the camera. Underneath in elaborate print it said:

Back home in Dungnastown at last

The day it was unveiled, Sister Gemma was so overwhelmed she said, 'He's like a God', and although the community knew she'd gone a bit daft, Bernard felt obliged to point out, 'We are all very proud of our connection with President Kennedy, Gemma, but there is only one God. No one resembles Him.'

In the silence that followed Bernard's gentle rebuke, Veronica was heard muttering to herself, 'Everybody's somebody and nobody's anybody ... death sees to that.'

Carmel now wondered about taking her advice and going up to her cell for a while. She then realised Bernard might walk in without knocking. She never wanted to see that woman again nor sleep in that cell again nor did she want to go without clarifying that leaving had more serious implications than grieving. She went over to the library table and wrote on an envelope:

Veronica love, I'm leaving. This is goodbye.
See you in heaven, God willing.

She embraced the old woman, kissed her and placed the note in her lap. She then left before Veronica had time to respond.

Out in the corridor, which looked out to the front and main entrance, Carmel saw one of the novices opening the heavy cast-iron gates as Bernard drove through in her black Volkswagen Beetle. Without hesitation she went down the garden to Martha, the only sister with keys to Bernard's office.

'I have to phone Tricia.'

Martha was taken aback, 'You have cause?'

'I need to talk to her now.'

'I could get the face ate off me for this,' Martha said as she handed Carmel a bunch of keys, showing her the one for the office.

'I'll explain later, Martha.'

Tricia took quite a while to lift the receiver.

'Trish? Are you free?'

'It's you, Carmel?'

'Yes.'

'I'm free enough.'

'Can you collect me?'

'What!'

'Now. I'm leaving for good, or bad.'

'You're not joking, are you?'

'I'm not.'

'Thanks be to God, it's about time.'

'Bring a cardigan, skirt, underwear, shoes. That's all I need.'

'An extra case?'

'No extra case. I came with nothing, I'll leave with nothing.'

Back in the garden Martha was on a cushioned kneeler hand-weeding onion sets. Carmel decided directness was the best way, 'I'm leaving, Martha. Trish will be here in an hour.'

It was as though Martha hadn't heard. She kept on weeding for about a minute then pushed herself to her feet with the kneeler handles. Rubbing one hand off the other, she accepted the keys. Her face said it all and when she spoke, her voice even more so. As she walked towards the polytunnel she suddenly seemed to have the walk of an older woman. They drank tea and talked. Martha knew it was pointless trying to dissuade her and had too much experience to ask about the whys and wherefores.

It was their longest tea break in two years, full of silences and sighs.

'No smidgeens of doubt girl?'

'None, I'm leaving.'

'You'll be missed, badly. You'll bid us farewell.'

'There won't be time. You do that for me, Martha.'

'You've no notion at all how much you're loved here.'

'Mother Bernard Barrett?'

'Bernard above all, maybe. That poor woman has creels and creels of trouble.'

The instinct to quote Francis de Sales occured to Carmel: 'Those who love to be feared fear to be loved'. She repressed the temptation by saying, 'We all have troubles.'

The back door from the scullery opened. Tricia appeared in the garden, holding Isabel by the hand. The child broke free, running down the flagged sandstone path and calling out Carmel's name. They came out of the polytunnel. As they watched Tricia approaching, Martha said, 'Your sister's the quare glamour puss this evening.'

'She makes a lot of herself,' Carmel said and went to her cell. She was changed and in the main hall by the time Martha and Tricia came in from the garden. There was awkward emotion at the massive front doors. Martha moved first by taking Carmel's face in her two hands and saying, as she kissed her forehead for the first and probably the last time, 'God bless you, child, I'll think of you and pray for you.'

'And I for you Martha, and I'll visit.'

'The ones that lave seldom do.'

'I will.'

On the way to Spanish Point, Isabel on Carmel's knee was so full of childish questions, rambling stories and non sequiturs that she wore herself out quickly and fell asleep. Carmel bent down to smell the child's hair. It brought back an immediate memory of their mother and childhood.

'What a wonderful thing a child is.'

'She's all that and a tyrant along with it.'

'You're joking me, Trish, this beautiful wee thing?'

'Ball and chain, still suckling at three.'

'Oh that's too long!'

After a few minutes' silence, Tricia asked,

'Do you want to talk?'

'Not really.'

'Too painful?'

'Much.'

'That's a very real person, the Martha one. I couldn't place her accent?'

'Cavan.'

'Of course.'

After a silence, Tricia said, 'Probably why she's down here.'

'What is?'

'The fire.'

'What fire?'

'You don't know?'

'Nothing.'

'Back during the war, there was a fire in their Cavan convent, a primitive brigade in the town, the convent an inferno. They could hear the nuns on their knees praying in the hall and the children screaming upstairs. Some of them jumped from three storeys. Thirty-five of them were burned.'

There was a long silence as Carmel remembered Martha in the garden: *That's one story I'll never tell.*

'Martha must have been a novice then,' Carmel said. 'God help her.'

'God did help her and all the nuns. *They* got out, every one of them. They buried what was left of the 35 children, arms and legs mostly, in one grave, wee ones as young as five and six. There was an enquiry. Faulty wiring they said. Back then no one dared say crazy nuns, everyone thought it though.'

Carmel was glad of the dark in the car. 'That's a cruel word to use about something so terrible.'

'What one would you use?'

'There's no word for something so awful, but I know the nuns weren't praying in the hall while children burned upstairs. That's gross, utterly unbelievable.'

After a silence Tricia said, 'Flann O'Brien was secretary to the inquiry. He thought otherwise.

In Cavan there was a great fire
Judge Mc Carthy was sent to inquire
It would be a shame if the nuns were to blame
So it had to be caused by a wire.'

During the silence that followed Carmel put the back of her hand up to her chin to stop the tears from dripping down and waking Isabel and thought, I'm going to find work and apply to the medical missionaries. I will not live longer than I have to with this sister of mine.

After a few miles Tricia said, 'You're going to get a bigger shock than Rip Van Winkle.'

Carmel hesitated before answering, aware that her voice might be thickened with emotion.

'Good or bad?' She asked.

'Hard to say. We've grown up, the whole country's profoundly different. The North is bloody chaos and the church is out of sync with most, if not *all* the young people.

᠀

I T WAS well into midsummer when Carmel spotted an ad. It had a telephone number and looked promising. She showed it to Tricia who read it aloud, her voice slowing as she read:

Responsible female urgently required in border town for ailing wife and mother. Must be willing to do light housework and help nurse occasionally. The care of a school-going boy will be part of the duties.

She continued to stare at the ad blinking and then said, 'I'd swear that's Des Grogan married to our cousin, Maura, Maura Quinn, remember?'

Carmel had a faint memory of her cousin long ago as a child. She was a professed nun when Maura had married Grogan.

'But how can you—?'

'Maura's got diabetes. She's not a well woman and Grogan's an undertaker. They've a wee lad a few years older than Isabel. Let's phone.'

As she dialled she lit a cigarette and said, 'I'm guessing but almost certain.'

Tricia listened, began to smile and nod. She then became serious as she asked about her cousin, saying every now and then, 'Oh dear, oh dear me. Oh poor Maura, oh God help her and poor you. I'd no idea. And when will your doctor have these results? Let's hope indeed, Desmond. I've been remiss about keeping in touch, but you know yourself, life, life, life! Hard to keep everything and everyone in mind.'

She then went on to explain how Carmel had left the enclosed community, was provisionally booked into Cork, saw the ad and was now looking for work until September.

'She's here beside me; you can talk to her yourself.'

Carmel took the receiver and heard a reson-
ant male voice with a strong Cavan accent. It
made her name sound like Caramel.

He wanted to know how soon she could
start. She told him soon, almost immediately
if he wanted.

'The sooner the better, Caramel. It's a godsend you seen my ad.'

It was indeed, Carmel thought later, a kind
of godsend. She would in a sense be working
within the kinship of family, but realised she
would miss the closer kinship of Isabel and
Tricia. Isabel was now weaned, but Tricia was
Tricia and, like most other people, liked having
her house to herself. She had her work, and
good work it was, no matter how she
shrugged. She knew from village talk that
Tricia was held in very high esteem, never
pressed people for money and was more than
solicitous about single mothers. Nonetheless a
change might be good for both of them.

Tricia had packed a large case with almost
unworn clothes and put it in the boot, despite
Carmel's protests.

'I don't need them, Trish.'

'Wear them and stop being nunny!'

On the long journey from Spanish Point to Ballinahone, Tricia said, 'By the way I put your bank account details and cheque book in the side sleeve of the case. Keep them where Desmond won't see them. If he thought you'd money he'd pay you next nothing.'

'How do you know that?'

'I'm guessing. He's pure Cavan. They're always on the make, trust no one, not even themselves!'

When Carmel blinked and frowned, Tricia laughed and said, 'I'm joking, Sis. Cavan jokes are neck-and-neck with Kerry ones. It just means they're cute, country hoors, that's all.'

As the Volkswagen approached Ballinahone, Carmel saw a large corner building at the end of the town. On the second storey they saw a name chiseled on black marble, highlighted by gold lettering:

DESMOND GROGAN

FUNERAL DIRECTOR

Carmel was very taken by the building, which had once been a Munster and Leinster bank premises, a three-storey cut-stone house with a long garden sloping down to a small tributary flowing towards Lough Erne. She could see apple, plum and pear trees and a copper beech mid-garden in glorious, midsummer plumage.

Desmond Grogan opened the hall door, a thin, slightly stooped man of middle height, fine skinned with a deep voice, good-looking with brown eyes that had a startled way of darting from face to face as though something unpleasant had been said about him or was about to be said. When talking, he had a habit of dropping the side of his mouth slightly before inclining his head for a response.

They were upset to find their cousin Maura very ill, so jaundiced, so deep asleep they agreed not to waken her. They sat at her bedside, talking in low voices. It was a nineteenth-century brass double bed brought down two months ago at the start of her illness. Desmond explained what didn't have to be explained.

'This room,' he whispered, 'was the bank parlour. Thon marble fireplace and fire bowl were here when my father bought it during the war.'

They responded appropriately, looking at the purple hearth-rug depicting kittens playing with a ball of wool and a floor covered with mock parquetry linoleum. The walls were hung with sepia, photographic portraits of Grogan grandees. Two especially distinguished family members were pointed out by Desmond, a cross-looking parish priest with Gladstone whiskers and an even crosser-looking man in a wig.

'That's Alec,' he whispered. 'A judge in the jungle somewhere back in the Empire days, Sir Alec Grogan, an awful man to hang cannibals. No mercy. It was all wrote up in an English newspaper after he died.'

There were no female relatives memorialised. The wallpaper hadn't been changed for a hundred years. Two upright armchairs faced the fireplace. In the high, expansive bow window looking west there was a Monaghan sofa, a sort of carved, mahogany day-bed covered in a Turkish fabric of faded splendour. It got the morning sun and looked down on the sloping garden. The old bank office was rented to a chemist, Mr Maurice Ferguson. Desmond dropped his voice and added, almost apologetically, 'a Protestant gentleman.' The basement was, he said, unused except for the deep-well pump that supplied house and yard. The water was crystal clear and always cold.

Maura opened her eyes. She seemed blind. The skin of her lips was raw and split. She closed her eyes again and went into what seemed a deep, snoring coma. Tricia felt her pulse, picked up and read the prescription tablets on the bedside table.

'You have a district nurse?' she asked.

'Moya Martin, she comes twice a day now.'

'And at night?'

'I sleep on that sofa.'

Tricia nodded and indicated that they should leave quietly.

No one wanted to talk about the obvious. The sisters admired the proportions of the kitchen, the old, cast-iron Esse cooker, the high ceiling, the usefulness of the pulley line draped with sheets. The walls were the colour of the tea and the brown scones being served by Tess Bastible who came daily for a few hours. Her husband Ollie drove the hearse and helped Desmond in the morgue.

They could hear the faraway sound of Isabel laughing. They went with their teacups to the high kitchen window. They could see their cousin's son Frank pushing Isabel on a swing hung from a branch of the copper beech. She shrieked with excited delight at every push.

'Happy cousins,' Carmel said and asked his age.

'Eight, goin' on nine,' Desmond said with what sounded like a break in his voice.

Tricia then asked the question that could no longer be avoided.

'The tests, Desmond, was your doctor in touch?'

'I'll tell no lie,' he said. 'It's bad news, not good at all, to be honest.'

'But he told you?'

'He did, he did. "The worst news," he said. "The very worst news of all."'

There was a silence before he spoke again.

'And what do you think of her yourself, at the minute, Patricia?'

'She's dying, Desmond.'

He seemed shocked by her directness.

'Would you say that?'

'Yes. But not obviously in pain yet.'

'No. True enough, true enough. Could you put a time on?'

'Soon.'

'How soon?'

Tricia shrugged and opened her hands.

'Unless she asks for water I wouldn't offer it.'

His face fell apart. When he looked as if he was about to cry, both sisters moved to touch or embrace him. He turned away suddenly and left the kitchen. They were looking out the window again through misted eyes watching the children when Carmel said, 'God help him and that poor boy.'

'Yes it's hard. Very hard. I'd no notion it was so serious.'

'You seemed very blunt there, Trish?'

'It's the best way. The doctor told him but he won't take it in. I think we should offer to stay on; he looks exhausted.'

'We?'

'I can control the pain if it gets bad through the night. She's not long for this world.'

They stayed. Desmond was genuinely grateful for their nursing and emotional support, especially for his son. Maura was dead, waked and buried within a week. An undertaker from Cavan town handled the funeral arrangements. There was then the question of Carmel working on until September. Desmond talked about light housework and maybe helping out in the office.

More importantly, Carmel was aware of the way her cousin's death had affected the boy. He was so stunned he seemed unable to eat or talk. Remembering their own mother's death, she felt that to leave now would be unthinkable until he adjusted to the corrosion of grief. There was no question of her staying in the house. She would find lodgings and come to the house after early Mass each morning, then make herself useful until evening. Desmond was more than agreeable to this. The payment offered was meagre but not mean. It covered her digs and left a few notes over.

It was difficult to talk on the house phone. Carmel went to a public booth at the weekends to catch Tricia before going out. Mostly she was lucky.

She mentioned that Frank was still grieving deeply after two weeks. He kept to his room and ate almost nothing. What worried Carmel most was how very anaemic he looked, almost like a Belsen child.

'Bring your own dinner up to him and offer him the odd bite. Plenty of lamb's liver and spinach. See if you can get that into him. Do his eyes remind you of anyone? It's struck me since.'

'They are familiar.'

'Mamma's, very like.'

'Yes, you're right.'

'So you quite like it up there?'

'It's going well. I've got to know lots of people in the digs and shopping for the house. They're very different to people around home, colder.'

'It's Ulster, love. Contagion from that crowd above. Rough and loud. Apart from the anaemia, how is he otherwise?'

'Ashamed now because he's bedwetting and his pillow's damp from crying.'

'Oh dear, poor child, poor you.'

'No, I'm glad to be here and it's getting better. I got a response yesterday.'

'You did?'

'Told him not to worry, that I sometimes wet the bed. That made him almost laugh and say, "I don't believe you, Auntie Carmel."'

'"Auntie Carmel", that's progress! And Desmond?'

'He's coping well. Almost normal, back to business.'

'Not much choice, has he, with perishable stock!'

Carmel took a deep breath.

'Trish you say really strange things sometimes and he's not one bit the way you said he'd be.'

'What way did I say he'd be?'

'A cute Cavan man.'

'Surely I said "hoor".'

Carmel went silent. Then coldly, 'Probably.'

'Oh don't be so tight-arsed, Sis, that was a throwaway nothing. Cavan and Kerry jokes are on a par.

'Well I know he sends no bills till people are well over their grieving and that's two years, he says.'

'That *is* a magnanimous … undertaking!'

'You've been drinking, Trish?'

'No more than usual on a wet Saturday evening with nowhere to go.'

'I'll phone next weekend.'

'I'm glad things are going well for you. Truly.'

'Bye Trish.'

'Bye love.'

Talking to Tricia could be unsettling. Sometimes she was quirky, querulous and irreverent about almost everything.

Like that growing up, knowing, making fun

of what others took seriously and using words that didn't have to be used. Tight-arsed. That was a rude one Carmel had never heard. Most likely American. It sounded American. What made it specially annoying was she could touch on a nerve of truth in an uncanny way that made Carmel withhold things she knew would be dismissed with casual irony. What she'd told Tricia on the phone was true. Desmond never invoiced the grieving till their grieving was well over. That he judged to be about two years. Word of this credit he maintained attracted abnormal funeral traffic and a more than normal amount of book debt. He spoiled it then by saying what she did not tell Tricia, 'Bad debts are rare in this trade. People'll borrow, beg or steal to pay for buried kin.'

The following day the phone rang. A call from Spanish Point, a small childish voice on the line, 'It's me, Isabel, I miss you Auntie Carmel an awful lot.'

'And I miss you too sweetheart and love you an awful lot.'

'When are you coming down to see us?'

'Whenever I can.'

'When?'

'I'll let you know.'

Tricia then came on the line.

'Sorry for being cranky last night. I was out of sorts.'

'I'd never have guessed!'

'By the way, there's more paperwork here from Cork.'

'Send them on.'

'Take care love, keep in touch.'

As the weeks passed, Frank stopped bed-wetting and asked her one day if she'd like to know a secret.

'Are you certain,' she asked, 'you want to share it?'

'I think so.'

'You won't regret it?'

'I won't. It's about Dad. His nickname is Dessie the Drac.'

'That's no great secret. Where did you hear it?'

'At school.'

'And who said it?'

'Boys, sometimes they say it and say it and say it.'

'Chant it?'

'Yes.'

'Why?'

'I don't know. They just pick on me.'

'Pay no heed to them.'

'I don't. That makes them worse.'

Dessie the Drac. If aware of his nickname Desmond never alluded to it. He did have a slight resemblance to Peter Cushing from what she remembered of a Dracula film she'd seen in Mallow before entering the convent, but there was nothing sinister about his teeth when he smiled. Ballinahone, like most other small towns, had no end of nicknames. Meagan the garage owner had the worst. One morning passing through the yard with Frank on her way to the garden with a basket of washing, Meagan had his head under the bonnet of the old Chrysler hearse when she heard him mutter, 'This old fucker of a hearse is fucked, Dessie. You need a new one badly.'

When well down the garden, she asked Frank who the man was.

'He owns a garage. He's called The Fucker Meagan.'

Carmel was sorry she'd asked and heard herself say, 'You don't have to use words like that, Frank.'

'Everyone calls him that.'

'That doesn't make it right, though he does seem a coarse type of person.'

Later when she asked Desmond about Meagan he didn't mention the nickname but said, 'He's well able to get parts, the same Meagan. Can't be bothered, just wants to sell me a new hearse, a carried-away auld cod with his pre-war Bentley Continental. Have you seen it?'

'The big cream car in the show window?'

'That's it, hires it out for weddings, always askin' me to go for a spin. I wouldn't plaze him; brags about how you can hear the dashboard clock at ninety. So I asked him, "Does that make you any happier, Packie?" He got the rough tongue out then, a loud, bad-tempered thick and a carried-away auld cod as crooked as they come hereabouts!'

Desmond didn't socialise much or drink in the town, though every Saturday evening he'd pour a half tumbler of malt whiskey in the kitchen and drink it straight, very slowly, while Carmel and Frank drank cocoa to keep him company. That was when he sometimes told cracker jokes or shaggy-dog stories so protracted she became uneasy about the punch lines.

Self-conscious about her poor sense of humour, she sometimes laughed too soon. What she did listen to with fascinated horror was his account of the burying of an IRA suspect informer.

'One night, four years back,' he said, 'the big door knocker woke me sudden, and a wild, windy night it was. Winter. I knew the man well. Local fella, the shouter McIntyre. "We've a dead doubtful in the van, Dessie." "Doubtful?" says I. "An informer … maybe?" "Who is he?" says I. "Sugar Mac Caw … a Protestant republican too sweet to be wholesome … they say he runs with the hare and hunts with the hounds." "And does he?" says I. "Sure who knows? We take orders and ask no questions. We need your help. Have you coffins in stock?" "Plenty," I said.

'There was six of them and a wee, fuzzy-headed priest in the middle of them always at Sinn Féin functions with his big chrome accordion singin' republican songs, a class of mascot priest. "No fancy parlour stuff," they said, "your chapest coffin."

'They lifted him out of a Ford transit. He'd a neat hole in his head … his eyes wide open and his low teeth stuck out like a monkey's. Oh a sad lookin' sight. We coffined him quick. When I asked again about what "doubtful" meant, they said, "They're near certain sure he's an informer but not dead sure if you get me. That's why we had to have the priest and the coffin. He could be dug up in 2016 and get a martyr's funeral and a statue when the whole story comes out."

'Poor Sugar. The Protestant provo who got a Catholic funeral He could be a class of hero in the heel of the hunt. It could be one of them big dodgy boys on the telly fingered him to cover his own back. No one knows the ins and outs of that bloody crowd.'

'Are you anyway involved, Desmond?' asked Carmel.

'Me! … You're coddin' me?'

'Did you bill them two years later?'

'Invoice! The IRA Incorporated! Not a penny offered or asked. I know the wee accordion priesty lad gets backhanders for that class of night shift. He drives a Saab car – all good Catholics, them lads. I seen all the top fellas on telly once, their tongues down to their chins for communion. Turn your stomach to watch them.'

'That's a terrible thing to say, Desmond!'

'What?'

'Offensive and unfair to judge another's motives for receiving communion.'

Desmond hung his head, blinked, shrugged and then agreed through the side of his mouth that 'maybe, yes, it was a bit, yes'.

The office work was not complex. It involved advising local radio and the local and national papers about funeral arrangements, then getting in touch with the church to find out about removal and funeral mass times. The church looked after graveyard details. She had to check the special debt ledger occasionally and advise debtors when payment was due. Desmond had a box of pre-signed postcards printed on elegant grey paper with a matching envelope, worded, she suspected, by a local journalist.

Dear

Regretfully the time for remuneration has arrived. We would be obliged if you could call to our office to reconcile the costs involved. We continue to be conscious of your loss but would be grateful if you could now defray our outstanding expenses without delay. Cash payments

would be appreciated but cheques are acceptable.
I remain yours in continuing sympathy,

Desmond Grogan
Funeral Director

If debtors called, Desmond had directed her to have all cheques made out to cash unless the debtor insisted on naming him. This Carmel went along with, wondering why, and then hinted for an explanation.

'CASH,' he said, 'stands for Christian Association of Self Help.'

Then he winked. She knew from the wink it was a dishonesty of some kind and felt foolish about asking for more details.

'The taxman doesn't have to know about every penny. Them tax lads are in cohoots with the big fellas, the bankers and buildin' societies. They get away with daylight robbery, millions, but small men like me get taken to the cleaners, or less they look out for their selves.'

'You don't pay tax, Desmond?'

'As little as I can, like most everyone else.'

When he could see her frowning, he said, 'You'd be agin' that, Carmel?'

'I know nothing about business or tax.'

Carmel found him baffling and contradictory. Now and then there was a cash crisis about insurance, paying coffin makers or keeping the old hearse on the road, but the big office safe was, she knew, full of photocopied maps and deeds of ownership in his name, small farms of land and waste ground adjacent to the town.

She spent every spare minute in the garden or new glasshouse, growing and weeding vegetables and pruning the great variety of neglected shrubs and ornamental trees, feeling almost guilty about the pleasure this gave her. Desmond praised her work but had no eye, interest or understanding about what she was doing. Time went by so quickly she missed filling in the final application for her place in Cork medical faculty which required her to send on her birth cert and Leaving Cert with a strict emphasis on the deadline for delivery. She had glanced at it presuming it to be a further notification or rubber stamping of acceptance.

It was early September. Frank was back at primary. She enjoyed walking out the Armagh Road to meet him after school. Most evenings, if requested, she helped him with homework. That was congenial. He was a clever, mannerly boy with an unusual flair for both languages and mathematics. Now and then her honours Irish was too rusty for everyday words like spade, rope, pitchfork or staircase. It was agreeable to look up Father Dinneen's dictionary and recognise what was forgotten. Were all those teenage years of serious study and the summers in a Gaeltacht the dead end of a dying tongue? No one in the convent used Irish except for the rosary now and then or the saint's hymn on St Patrick's Day and, of course, occasionally the national anthem with its warlike images and Anglophobia. She was pleased to hear one day that her growing affection for the boy was reciprocated.

Desmond told her Frank had reacted to a bully from Casement Park who had mocked her as 'thon auld nun wan works at your dead shop'. Frank had snapped back, 'She's not auld, she's not a nun and it's a morgue not a shop and she works in the office.'

'Oh, he can tongue,' Desmond added, 'and gets the temper out the same as the mother, if he takes the notion.'

Tricia knew Carmel had been Sister Martha's helper in the preparation of two nuns for burial in the convent graveyard. She had warned her on the first trip up to Ballinahone, 'Be careful not to give him the faintest whiff of that or he'll have you up to your oxter in corpses.'

That, she now realised, was possibly true. A lot of old people died over the winter months. If a flu epidemic struck, Desmond had to work long hours with Ollie Bastible. Ollie was nicknamed Bonkers by the local intelligentsia, but he was a man of parts. As an offshoot of the funeral trade he wrote remembrance anniversary 'poems' to order for the *Anglo-Celt* and a serial called *The Ghost of Derrylea*. It ran for years and was still in great demand. The poems, Carmel thought, were awful beyond description, the weekly serial even worse. It was widely read and popular with the pastoral community ('Oh, he's the quare boy with the pen').

Carmel got on well with both Ollie and his wife Tess who continued to help in the house four hours a day on weekdays. Tess enjoyed the cup of tea and gossiping about this, that and the other, most of it harmless enough, but one or two details Carmel found both distasteful and almost incredible.

Tess told her, 'Cathcart the draper sometimes laves them weemen dummies in the windy without a stitch on them betimes and wee lassies and caudies on their way to school can see all. So one mornin' Maura sent Dessie over to make a complent. He didn't want to go but he had to. Cathcart come out and says, "Tell you what I'll do, Desmond, I'll turn their arses to the street. That won't give offence," says he, "because one arse is the same as the next." Coorse he's a black Protestant and said thon for badness, but then he'd be sour on account of Desmond's loft.'

'Desmond's loft?'

'Aye.'

Tess hesitated, then realised she had to elaborate. She went on to explain that there was a padlocked loft above the morgue full of trousers, skirts and shoes removed from corpses before the satin coverlet with the embroidered cross was stapled up to the joined hands clasping a rosary beads. Men's underpants and women's knickers were not removed. That was deemed improper.

'People,' she said, 'whispered about it in pubs. At funerals as the coffins were being loaded into the hearse or lowered into the ground they'd maybe think to theirselves, "I wonder has that boyo or that poor auld lassie to face Saint Peter in Long Johns or knickers or maybe God Almighty himself or The Blessed Virgin and maybe a clatter of saints after that?" It's a holy fright to think about the lek.'

'You're not making this up, Tess?'

'Look at the two them in the best of black wool or gabardine trousers, belongin' to auld parish priests mostly. Ollie has no end of them and soft black leather shoes or boots. They wouldn't dare wear anythin' belongin' to a local body. That'd be copped right away. A Pakistani man comes up from Limerick once a year with a big van and buys the leftovers.'

She had no reason to disbelieve any of this. Both Desmond and Ollie were always in black trousers, socks and fine leather boots or shoes, dressed as it were for business, something she'd rather not think about and certainly would not ask about. If these wearables were going down to rot in a grave it could hardly be described as stealing. On the other hand it was grossly disrespectful to the dead. Knowing about it made her uncomfortable. She would have to broach it sometime.

Every now and then she imagined herself as a pre-med in Cork at the age of twenty-seven going on twenty-eight. All the bright young students, a decade younger with their youthful irreverence and casual sex. She would stick out like a carbuncle and be treated as such. It was so unappealing she excluded it from her thoughts until one evening she opened a formal circular to find she was too late. The date had passed. Her acceptance had been cancelled. She phoned the registrar in panic. A voice told her.

'We got no details by registered post – your birth cert, your Leaving Cert. We presumed you'd changed you mind. I' m afraid your place is gone.'

She would have to apply again, wait another year. Instead of disappointment she felt a kind of relief as though she'd thrown off a burden, escaped some future threat or anxiety.

When she told Tricia there was such a protracted silence she had to ask, 'Are you still there? Trish?'

Tricia's voice came rasping down the line,

'I hope you're joking me.'

'You sound angry?'

'I'm flabbergasted. That's the kind of thing happens to me, not you. Don't tell me you forgot?'

'I didn't read the small print about sending on certs. I presumed I was in, accepted.'

'Have you any idea what a disaster this is? Young ones'd cut throats to get your chance if short of points! What in God's name happened? Is it accidentally on purpose? Are you smitten by Desmond Grogan? You're in love with his son?'

'Of course I love the child.'

'Then you fancy the father too.'

'That's silly logic.'

'Is it? You threw away your life once, don't do it again. God in heaven, what an opportunity missed. You'd have sailed through. You'd have had a life. What are you going to do now?'

'I haven't thought about it.'

'You have. You're staying on with the funeral director. Does he know, have you told him?'

'What gives you the right to be so nosy and sarky?'

'I care about you, Sis, but I don't know what's in your head. And I'm not sure you know either. I'm disappointed for you, very.'

When Desmond proposed a year later, she went on a special retreat to the Graan Monastery near Enniskillen where she was advised by a Passionist priest to accept Desmond's proposal. It was, he told her, all quite in order.

With great circumspection she brought up the subject of the locked loft and confiscated clothes. Desmond inclined his head and talked through the right-hand side of his mouth, embarrassed. He agreed with her that he was not a poor man and didn't have to resort to what she called 'a great indignity'.

In his defence he told her his father had done this removal of lower clothes all his life. He'd grown up with it and thought it a normal part of the business. He assured her the practice would be discontinued. It was during a pause following this promise that she wondered where he had been schooled. He was not stupid but seemed to make such strangely stupid decisions that she asked him suddenly.

'Where were you schooled, Desmond?'

'Saint Pat's, Cavan.'

'Did you like it there?'

'Well enough.'

'You did your Leaving Cert?'

'Aw God no, Caramel. The auld fella took me home to help after Inter Cert.'

'And how did you get on at Inter?'

'Rightly enough at maths and science, but a woeful speller, still am.'

'You had no chance, Desmond.'

At the beginning his grammar and pronunciation grated. She was sometimes tempted to correct him, but knew this would be both pointless and insulting to a man of forty-four. Frank she corrected twenty times a day. He accepted her corrections without objection.

'You'll have him spakin' like a proper gentleman!' Desmond said with what she suspected was a mocking wink.

They had a quiet wedding after Easter. The Holy Land was too dangerous for their honeymoon. Carmel suggested Santiago de Compostela. Desmond's auctioneer brother Joe and wife Lillian flew out as witnesses and went on to Malaga.

While out there Desmond respected her

extreme nervousness and modesty. She returned a virgin but was pregnant by Christmas. Thereafter he assured her that sex was permitted during pregnancy. Carmel was less certain and asked her confessor, a local curate. He had a strong Mayo accent.

'Not sinful,' he advised, 'but far from ideal. We should be mindful at all times that none of God's creatures use congress during that time preceding parturition.' It was a matter, he said, for her own conscience and that of her husband's.

Carmel relayed this clerical opinion to Desmond.

'Part your what?' he asked.

'Parturition,' Carmel said, 'giving birth.' Desmond agreed with a reluctant shrug. She moved down to a pull-out divan in the living room which she loved for its high bow window, its view of the long, sloping garden.

Knowing Frank's ninth birthday was midsummer's day, Tricia phoned, inviting herself and Isabel up to celebrate. Carmel was more than delighted at the idea of the visit. Most exciting of all, Tricia would marvel at the miracle of her pregnancy which was now showing.

Frank was already booked in for a month's stay with Bean an Tighe O'Hara in Gweedore. She kept a two-storey house full of two-tier bunks for fourteen children. They came from all over the country. O'Hara's house had a great name for fun, food and discipline. Many of the children's parents booked into B&Bs or small hotels within a convenient radius so they could visit occasionally. Many spoke Irish in the home. For them talking to native speakers was like going back to a cultural past of endless fascination. And it worked both ways. The locals, small farmers, fishermen or contractors, were more than keen to correct an inflection, meaning or subtlety of words, sayings and sentence construction, especially if the parents involved were media, civil servants, politicians or professionals – very often people they'd seen on television.

Frank seemed to be looking forward to the month away.

Tricia arrived with Isabel in good time for the birthday party. In less than two years Carmel had got to know as many if not more townspeople and their children than Desmond. The kitchen was full of them and the cacophony and high octane screeching that accompanies such entertainments. When the candles were blown out for the third time to noisy singing and clapping, the adults retreated to the living room. Tess Bastible had brought an American niece and nephew and stayed on in the kitchen to keep order. When the children were collected or in bed, Desmond had to go out to buy gin and tonic, forgetting that Tricia never drank whiskey.

It was a mild, very beautiful midsummer's evening and still lightsome at eleven. They went down the garden and sat in a willow dome immersed in the smell of night stock and freshly cut grass. The swallows were high. It was, Carmel thought, an evening as close to absolute happiness as she had ever experienced. Tomorrow they would have a long drive up to Letterkenny, then on to Gweedore. It was arranged that Tricia and Isabel would travel with them. Perhaps they'd stay on for a day or two if the weather held to see Frank settled in.

The day after midsummer's day had a clear blue sky and was already hot, 70 degrees in the shade. The forecast promised continuing fine weather. When Tricia didn't come down, Carmel went up to the attic bedroom on the top floor with a breakfast tray. Tricia sat up in bed and begged Carmel not to open the curtains.

'Sorry, Sis, I have a real bitch of a headache. Just tea. Nothing to eat.'

Carmel got her two Anadins and sat on the side of the bed while Tricia swallowed the tablets, sipped tea and lit a cigarette.

'Are you well enough to travel, Trish?'

'In that heat? Could we postpone it?'

'The sandwiches are made, lemonade in the cooler box, the hotel in Dunfanaghy booked for us tonight. Frank and Isabel are raring to go. So am I.'

'Then go, Sis. This brute of a headache takes ages to ease. I'll hold the fort here.'

It was near midday when they got away. After Letterkenny and three hours of steady driving, they pulled in to a lay-by and had the banana sandwiches and lemonade. Frank said he wasn't hungry and seemed unusually quiet. When Carmel asked him was he all right he nodded his head in a way she read as negative.

'Are you car sick, sweetheart? It's nothing to be ashamed of.'

He shook his head.

'A little perhaps? Let's go for a walk.'

They went down through bracken and heather into a glen. There was a small, shallow river with bright water running noiselessly over brown stones, swallows so high their cries could scarcely be heard. They seemed like black insects in a yellowing sky. Carmel and Isabel sat with their feet in the water. Frank joined them, almost unwillingly it seemed. No, he said, there was nothing wrong.

Across the river they could see an old woman stooping as she built clamps of turf. She was with a boy and a girl, probably her grandchildren, all of them barefoot in worn work clothes. Late, Carmel thought, very late to be out working in the bog, but then fine weather was a chance not to be missed, the misery or warmth of winter determined by a few fine summer nights and days. There would be no Aga in their open hearth. In the distance they could see the cabin and far beyond it the black outline of The Twelve Bens. The old woman's posture was uncannily like Martha's and, watching her, Carmel was reminded how one summer's evening from the arched window halfway up the convent staircase she could make out Martha with a torch, stooping here and there in the half-dark to top up jam jars of beer waste to drown the ubiquitous slugs.

'Hand to mouth and the clatter of childer … that's no life. This garden here's paradise forby that torture.'

That image and attitude of Martha's had stayed, reminding her now of this old woman who stood suddenly and straightened, hands on her hips to ease the pain of backache.

Whether it was the effect of the water or the absolute silence of the bog, their soft western accents carried odd words and phrases, the old woman's more clearly than the children's.

'Tired, granny?'

'So I am love. This work racks my back … worse again, my heart.'

Then she talked on in a low voice that was over-called by a curlew.

After a long pause the girl said something that sounded like, 'Dada.'

And then clearly, 'He's my son, girsha, more's the shame!'

Then silence again. Their father, Carmel wondered? The old woman's son? Was he glugging beer in a pub or off with another woman? And her daughter-in-law, their mother? Home with small ones or in hospital and sick unto death? Or maybe dead itself? What could the future hold for her but continuous hardship till the release of death and the ease of hereafter.

And her grandchildren? What kind of lives awaited them? Emigration and all that implied. Instinctively, protectively, Carmel put her arms around Isabel and Frank and as she did the old woman turned for the first time to see the young woman across the river with two children. She smiled and waved. Carmel returned her greeting in kind, conscious of the lovely children on either side of her and even more so of the child in her womb. It was too far to call out, and anyway the old woman had begun building the base of another clamp. Time. Time. Time. Relentless work for millions and millions. Now and long ago and forever more. It struck her that people passing in cars would see this old woman working late in the bog with her grandchildren and imagine it a scene of pastoral, enviable happiness, like a painting called *The Gleaners* in the convent dining room which hung alongside another called *The Angelus*.

They made their way back to the car. After a mile or so she switched from dim to full headlights. As she did so Frank suddenly broke, crying with such gulping intakes of breath that she pulled over to a lay-by and stopped. Unnerved by his emotion, she put both arms around him and asked, 'What is it love, what is it? Tell us.'

'I don't want to go. I'm afraid.'

'Of what?'

'I don't know. I'm sorry. I don't know.'

Then Isabel said, 'Auntie Carmel, he told me he's lonely and he doesn't want to go. He wants to be at home with you and Uncle Desmond.'

They sat for half an hour in the growing dark. She knew talking would be useless. This sudden grief had more to do with Maura's death than facing strange children in a Gaeltacht. Then he said, 'I'll go next year, promise.'

There was no question of driving on. She went as far as the next village and phoned O' Hara's in Gweedore and the hotel in Dunfanaghy to cancel.

Both said, 'No problem, Mrs Grogan.'

Not to waken Tricia or Desmond, she cut the engine, freewheeled and parked the car on the Armagh Road beside the garden door. It was 3.30 a.m. On the bunch of car keys there were keys to the garden entrance and the basement door. Frank was dozing on the back seat. Isabel, in the front, was in a deeper sleep. As she carried her through the hall she heard, or imagined she heard, Desmond's low voice high up in the house. Surely not? She stood in the dark listening. Then Tricia's unmistakable smoker's laugh. Her head in a maze of imagining and disbelief, she opened out the divan bed, laid Isabel on it and went out to the hall. For a couple of minutes nothing but the ticking of an Austrian wall clock and the pounding of her heart. Her breathing had quickened. There it was again, Tricia's low laugh. Going back down to the car to fetch Frank, her breathing became so shallow she had to stop and sit on a garden bench.

A voice in her head kept saying, 'It couldn't be true, it couldn't', but as she walked on down to get Frank the voice said, 'You know it's true, you know it'. She led Frank by the hand as he half walked, half stumbled up to the living room. She undressed him to his vest and underpants, placed him beside Isabel on the divan and covered them both. He fell into a deep sleep almost immediately.

She began negotiating the stairs, avoiding the creaky ones till she reached the first landing. It then became very obvious. Desmond had gone up to join Tricia in the attic bedroom in Maura's old brass bed. For a moment she was going to go back down, but the fascination of the grossly incredible drew her up silently to the third landing. And then up the small winding staircase to the attic landing. Again it was the huskiness of a smoker's laugh, and Tricia's voice saying, 'Desmond, you're a naughty, naughty boy. The judge and the parish priest look *very* cross. Should we cover them with towels?

This was followed by giggling and the creak of Desmond getting out of bed as he said something she couldn't catch. For about ten seconds her whole body flared with a burning sensation then cooled so suddenly she was aware of trembling as she suppressed the initial instinct to go flailing and screaming into what she knew she would find. There was no way she could imagine dealing with such profound betrayal. Tomorrow morning she'd look in their eyes to see what she could read. She went back down and settled herself on the Monaghan sofa in the bow window. Silence but for the breathing of the two children. The tears scalding down her cheeks lessened. As she began to repeat the Hopkins' mantra, she fell into a deep and merciful sleep.

It was birds that wakened her and light from the east filling the garden. How could the world be at once so beautiful and so ugly? She dressed quickly and pulled the curtains to keep the children from waking. She could hear someone in the kitchen, the familiar sound of water splashing into a kettle. She closed the living room door silently and then stood in the doorway of the hall that gave on to the kitchen. Tricia was in her creamy silk dressing gown wearing knickers but no bra. She was lighting a cigarette, her back to Carmel, who said quietly, 'Another beautiful day, thank God.'

Tricia dropped both cigarette and lighter as she uttered a startled sound, a rasping noise verging on a scream. This turned into a harsh smoker's cough that brought tears to her eyes and left her so breathless she was just able to say, 'You put the heart crossways in me, Sis. I thought you were in Dunfanaghy.'

'Frank got homesick – so choked up I thought he'd get unwell. We came home.'

'Of course, of course, that was sensible.'

As Tricia bent to pick up the cigarette and lighter, Carmel could see her breasts clearly and said, 'We got back around half three. I could hear you from down here.'

'What!'

'I said I could hear you from down here in the hall.'

'Oh God.'

'Not God, Trish, you and Desmond.'

As the kettle began to sing on the Aga, Tricia went over and sat at the table. She seemed hunched, almost shrunken, and for once at a loss for words. Eventually she said, 'It's terrible, I know, but these stupid things happen ... unplanned, accidental.'

Carmel did not reply. She moved to the back window and stood sideways looking out. Tricia could see the outline of her growing belly. Pregnancy made her seem, if anything, more beautiful.

'Sis, come over and sit, you have no idea how awful I feel.'

'I don't feel great myself.'

Tricia motioned to a chair beside her and said, 'Please.'

Carmel went over and sat opposite. Neither said anything till Tricia said, 'Say something … anything.'

After a hesitation Carmel said, 'May God forgive you, Trish.'

'What?'

'I said may God forgive … both of you.'

'Oh for Christ's sake, Carmel! What the hell has God got to do with it? It's your forgiveness I want, not His … it's you I'm begging from the bottom of my heart. I couldn't be sorrier … so stupid … so very, very, very stupid and it meant nothing, less than nothing.'

'Was what Judas did … nothing?'

In the protracted silence that followed they could hear Desmond coming out of the bathroom on the upper landing where Carmel imagined he would have cleansed his hands, penis and scrotum of dried semen and her sister's vaginal secretions. She thrust this revolting image from her mind by taking a deep breath.

'Remember when I suggested you pray with me for Dada?'

'What?'

'Remember what you said?'

'Why ask now?'

'It came into my head.'

'Not a clue. Something awful I suppose. Was it?'

'"I hope he's dead," you said, "and gone to hell".'

'That sounds likely enough. So?'

'I asked, could you not find it in your heart to forgive him.'

Tricia waited, watching Carmel's perfectly modelled lips, waiting for them to move, to elaborate.

'Don't taunt me – I'm so ashamed, I honestly can't remember.'

'You said, "Never".'

'Did I? And that's how you feel about me now, unforgiving?'

Silence. The face of a forlorn statue looking away and then, 'No, that would be wrong, but—'

Carmel had put her hands on the table to get up. Tricia put out her right hand to cover one of them, 'But what? What?'

It was a bit like the time in the convent chapel when Maeve Marron caught her in that unnerving grip as she confessed her love. From a glance she could see guilt or grief or something beginning to glaze Tricia's eyes. As she slowly withdrew her hand she heard, 'Say something. Scream at me. Get angry!'

'I'm ... numb, sick at heart and don't know what to say or think or feel or do or not do ... or stay or go or ... It's as if someone died belonging to us but, I don't know who ... me I think ... or you ... both of us ... or all three.'

'Oh for Christ's sake,' Trish muttered. 'It's not the end of the world. No one's died!'

She lit a cigarette, inhaling deeply, gathering courage to counter attack.

'It's just a silly mess ... mine ... maybe yours a bit! Did you have to leave his bed because you were pregnant? Priesteen advice, was it? Jesus! You could have stayed, spooned and fondled him, relieved him. You're a married woman! Sex is normal. You've got a licence!'

They heard Desmond's step creak on the staircase. Clearly he'd been listening. He hesitated in the hall before joining them in the kitchen. Carmel moved away from the table, staring back at him with revulsion and a sudden, violent hatred. What would he say? What could he say? His eyes were darting about avoiding hers. He was like a dog that had stolen the Sunday roast and been caught wolfing it. Incredibly he moved towards the table and sat opposite Tricia. Carmel continued staring at him with disbelief. Would he now tap the unset table as usual and expect her to set it, make him toast, boil him an egg as if nothing had happened? And if he did tap the table, what could she throw at him? She was beside the dresser. Near it there was a Sacred Heart on the wall. Not that, but maybe the old-fashioned ewer decorated with roses and ivy on the dresser top, just within reach. She heard him say, 'A great mistake, a misfortune. There was a share of drink on the job.'

Tricia now had her elbows on the table, her head in her hands, cigarette smoke curling from her fingers. She did not look up or speak. What a half-witted apology, she thought, 'on the job'.

Two innocents tripping into the snares of alcohol and adultery.

Isabel came into the kitchen looking sleepy and cross as Carmel turned to the window. She could see down to the yard where Ollie Bastible was talking to Meagan. The bonnet of the hearse was open. Meagan was shaking his head, mouthing casual curses and shrugging. Though she had never used the word in her life, she now heard herself say, slowly, deliberately, 'The Fucker Meagan's below in the yard. I'd say he wants you for the hearse.'

She did not look round to see his reaction as she heard him leave the kitchen. Isabel looked suddenly wide awake and said, 'Auntie Carmel, you said the *very* bad word!'

'Did I?'

'I heard you.'

Tricia opened her arms and said, 'Come here darling.'

She took Isabel on her knees, enclosing her in her arms, kissing her face, nose, eyes, ears and hair.

'Mammy your face is all wet! Why are you crying?'

'Because you were far, far away yesterday, love, and I was wondering what it would be like if you never came back, if I lost you forever.

I'd be so sad I'd die of a broken heart.'

Outside the hearse sputtered to life, back-fired like a rifle shot, then stopped.

The silence in the kitchen seemed so un-natural that Isabel put her hands on her mother's shoulders and pushed her away to read her face. She then looked over at her aunt and asked, 'Is it because Aunty Carmel sounded so cross and used *that* word?'

The question hung in the air unanswered and seemed likely to stay there until Carmel said, 'Yes, love, that's why. It was my fault. I see that now. Can *you* forgive *me*?'

Isabel looked baffled for a moment. Carmel then knelt and gestured with open arms. As the child ran to embrace her aunt, the sisters' eyes met.

Neither looked away.